T0196318

A Mermaid's Wink

Book One

The narrator is Venus Fly,
telling her story—
from the cold sea…

KAREN HALL

authorHOUSE®

AuthorHouse™
1663 Liberty Drive
Bloomington, IN 47403
www.authorhouse.com
Phone: 1 (800) 839-8640

© *2017 Karen Hall. All rights reserved.*

No part of this book may be reproduced, stored in a retrieval system, or transmitted by any means without the written permission of the author.

Published by AuthorHouse 03/10/2017

ISBN: 978-1-5246-6997-3 (sc)
ISBN: 978-1-5246-6996-6 (e)

Print information available on the last page.

Any people depicted in stock imagery provided by Thinkstock are models, and such images are being used for illustrative purposes only. Certain stock imagery © Thinkstock.

This book is printed on acid-free paper.

Because of the dynamic nature of the Internet, any web addresses or links contained in this book may have changed since publication and may no longer be valid. The views expressed in this work are solely those of the author and do not necessarily reflect the views of the publisher, and the publisher hereby disclaims any responsibility for them.

Prologue

{Venus Fly}
Something I found—
on sandy ground—
that I behold,
a chain of gold,
rusted and old.
I slip it on my neck,
deeming me a wreck—
with shaky hands—
and salty sands—
stuck to my scales.

Some skin peels—
and drops in flakes,
no matter my heart aches.
So much for me,
a mermaid that be,
"Venus Fly,"
wooing the sea—
with eyes enchanted.

"Lover," I said,
wishing to abed…

Introduction

Reader,
An ocean of surprise—
lies within my eyes—
in pages writ bold…

"Your hands hold—
this book sold,"
read on seashores,
the library,
else wherever any.

—Abana Fare

Chapter One

STORYTELLER, VENUS FLY

Tall Tale

{Storyteller}
(Venus Fly)

As storyteller,
reader,
I introduce I,
"Venus Fly."
I welcome each one,
my story begun…

Sat upon a rock,
basking awhile,
I brushed my long hair—
with utmost care,
straightening curls—
that turned to swirls—
of locks drawn wavy.
As is the sea,
that throws turbulent—
sentiment,
rocky waves, and brine—
that I call mine.

Tall Tale

{Storyteller Continued}
(Venus Fly)

By trade, reader,
I am a writer,
whom pen fiction told—
as my story enfold…

It was a breezy day—
in the middle of May—
whence my eyes beheld—
his hand I held.
Later, with grace—
we did embrace…

It happened near a wishing well.
I recall he wore a crown.
And I, awkward, slipped, fell down…
down the wishing well.
Falling, falling, till I fell—
in a spring of drink.

Tall Tale

{Storyteller Continued}
(Venus Fly)

Scrawls my ink,
"I swam lazily—
while the well-water became my sea."

East and west,
I had quest,
searching for royalty.
"But where was he?"
Not here,
nor there.
"Oh where…
where went my king?"

Later, from depths I did emerge,
feeling an urge—
to eat moss,
wet with a salty gloss.

Tall Tale

{Storyteller Continued}
(Venus Fly)

To a newfound rock,
I clung—
while rung—
the clock.
Then, I thunk—
if I drunk—
with eyelids sunk,
he might appear—
before me, near.

Wistful, I did wink,
whilst my heart did sink—
and "what had appear?"
"A merman's leer"—
with golden eyes—
before me, shone surprise.
Nostalgic, he then averted his stare—
and descended there,
sunken in depths of cold…

Tall Tale

{Storyteller Continued}
(Venus Fly)

Ago, in times past old,
my heart I would've sold—
just to hold—
his hand—
in waters grand.

Then I did view—
the sea navy blue—
and admired all around,
where weeds abound—
as a mermaid picked seaweed,
hoping to satiate her need.

Then, waiting to dine,
puckered my lips,
kissing a vine—
laced with flaky brine—
and salt deposits,
which I'd ate in bits.

Tall Tale

{Storyteller Continued}
(Venus Fly)

In retrospect, I noted—
my heart full of dread,
rolling on a "bed—
of roses,"
where once I'd abed.

The water near black,
I'd a sudden flashback:
whence I fell,
I tumbled swell,
down the darkened well.
"And saw doom," I spell.
At the bottom, I hum,
"I swum,
catching my breath—
with hands numb."

The waves turned rough.
I felt I had enough.

Tall Tale

{Storyteller Continued}
(Venus Fly)

Still, with blown bubbles,
I saw sands brush pebbles.

In waters deeper,
I breathe easier,
sucking in—
water from within—
my sea of ocean.
Then, I exhale—
with fishy lungs avail.

Lovesick,
I missed my fiancé,
whom dwelt out of the way.
I felt horrid dismay.
Then, a wound sore—
sudden bleeds,
cut by weeds,
where another fish feeds.

Tall Tale

{Storyteller Continued}
(Venus Fly)

I noticed thick brine in the sea,
caressing me,
leaving my shoulders foamy.

Then, breathing heavy,
larger bubbles did appear—
against my chest near...

"Bubbly," some call me—
in the sea—
with subtle curve.

If you observe—
a bubble in the sea,
you'll aware—
a magical glare,
transparent and clear,
as if a crystal ball could float around,
never seeming to touch ground.

Tall Tale

{Storyteller Continued}
(Venus Fly)

Teardrops afore me—
filled my sea—
with eyes watery.

Certain others did fill—
my ocean with shrill,
and catcall,
where verbal insult spills—
as bubbles fall from gills.
Such are "primitive fish."

Albeit mermaids grant wish,
still they can be barbaric,
erotic,
too tart and—
dangerous on land;
yet, even more tricky upon sand.
They're also "hard to hold."
And some are very old.

Tall Tale

{Storyteller Continued}
(Venus Fly)

"Mermaids, beware,"
I scold,
"don't turn my sea to mold."
Pay heed,
"I rule—
even if sour tongues drool."

"I'm Queen—
of waters seen.
My blood rather cold,
I'm one bold—
with eyes lit gold,
a figure curvy,
a dramatic story,
and fire on my tongue,"
dreary sung.

—Venus Fly

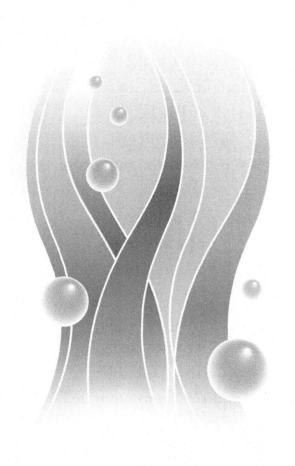

Chapter Two

SPOTLIGHT, ABANA FARE

Dear Reader,

"A Mermaid's Wink,"
writ in ink,
shares a tale—
of how I feel—
in my ocean of fantasy,
where I, a mermaid, just be—
beneath the words you see—
as you read me. . .

—Abana Fare

Tall Tale

{Storyteller}
(Venus Fly)

As my story evolves,
it involves—
a mermaid, that differs rare,
called, "Abana Fare."

She is timid—
with tremors—
and shaken horrors,
regarding her health.
A poor heart has she.
And wistful memory,
regarding "he,"
a merman named, "Ulder,"
a former lover.
She awaits his return—
with passionate yearn.
Spending her days—
in prayer,
wishing him back near.

Tall Tale

{Storyteller Continued}
(Venus Fly)

Between coral reefs and weeds,
Abana hides her needs—
while her heart bleeds.

"A bleeding heart,"
often she fall apart,
losing her composure,
unable to rhyme a measure—
and gasps with slanted posture.

Abana appears loose,
drinking juice—
from bitter seaweed—
she need.
Then, she swim sloppy, unusual,
to reach a rock above water level;
so she may forget—
her dismay and fret,
and dry her tail wet.

Tall Tale

{Storyteller Continued}
(Venus Fly)

Near an iceberg white,
with sunlight—
upon her sight,
she sun-bathes her raw tail—
under warmth to heal.

Seagulls come—
to hear her hum.
Abana sings to them,
"The beauty—
of birds scary—
I discovered here,
afore your wings soar."

She then whisper,
"Wilted flower—
found on a glacier—
brings sadness to my soul—
as my eyes roll."

Tall Tale

{Storyteller Continued}
(Venus Fly)

"The birds' hearts,"
she stole.
"The seagull's eye,"
she sigh,
"grows weary—
upon this day eerie."

Gloomy or dismal—
or just plain dull,
she expects bad weather;
beating rain-water,
falling like spears—
or crying icy tears—
as the clouds that break—
are those that make—
rainfall splatter and beat,
wetting traveler's feet.
However falls sleet,
her eyes wait to greet...

Tall Tale

{Storyteller Continued}
(Venus Fly)

…Ulder,
hoping romance—
would have another chance,
even at first glance.

As ruler of the sea,
reader,
most quickly flee—
whenever they spot me.
But "Abana Fare"—
seems to bear—
my position as despot—
without eyes rot.

She complains a lot—
about her poor health—
and lack of wealth.
And as a pauper,
she offers any favor.

Tall Tale

{Storyteller Continued}
(Venus Fly)

So I made her—
a "royal beggar,"
and every day she says,
"She's richer."

Many give her feed;
wild grown weed—
and kelp in bunch—
so she may have lunch.

Some throw coin shiny,
feeling sorry—
that she's a pauper—
and for a beggar—
not very proper.

But I find—
her teeth she not grind,
nor does she mind...

Tall Tale

{Storyteller Continued}
(Venus Fly)

…begging for treat—
from whomever she meet.
Such is life for her;
she not find it bitter.

For those passerby motley,
she give a soliloquy,
often holding a hat—
for tips to put in that.

She recount, soft-spoken,
with eyes green and golden…

{Expressed to Birds}
(Abana Fare)

"Birds," I chant,
"a wish I grant—
as my eyes enchant."

Tall Tale

{Expressed to Birds Continued}
(Abana Fare)

"Ask me any, please,
even a basket of strawberries!"
The birds request soft food—
with eyes brood.
So with my eyes,
kind and wise,
I will them bread—
so they are fed.

Once I say is said.
A loaf of bread—
now appear—
before the birds near.

Then, they ask for a cocktail.
So I, twisting my tail,
will a tiny umbrella—
in each glass of water.

Tall Tale

{Soliloquy}
(Abana Fare)

The birds are my friends—
as my heart mends…

They now fly away,
leaving me alone—
as shone.

And under sunshine,
I begin to whine…
My bones ache,
leaving heartache—
with misery—
in the sea…

My skin is bruised—
over cheap lotion used.
My nail polish flake,
leaving dirt in my lake.

Tall Tale

{Soliloquy Continued}
(Abana Fare)

Sure I'm pretty,
but you'd never know—
cause I lost—
a tooth and dost—
my lips look frost.

My complexion appears red,
burnt I dread.
Should've worn hat—
with rim, I spat.

Tired, my eyes shun—
the scorching sun.
With eyes weep,
I dive, swimming deep,
searching seas of cold—
for he, a bit old;
the one foretold—
would his arms hold…

Tall Tale

Wistful,
ago,
my admirer,
Ulder,
became my adored lover.
He, my betrothed,
whom had prior engagement.
Where now has he went?
Alone, time I've spent.

Swimming ahead,
I spot vegetation rooted.
Above it I sped.
But somehow weeds—
entangled the tip of my tail—
that now bleeds.
I try to shake it,
all of it,
as ought.

Tall Tale

{Soliloquy Continued}
(Abana Fare)

But however sought,
I cannot—
easily break free.

The weeds, terribly,
are now all over me:
around my waist shows;
about my chin and nose;
wrapped around my arms,
fingertips and palms.

Tangled about my stomach—
and neck,
the weeds do wreck—
my freedom,
I hum.

Trapped in weeds—
and bitter seeds…

Tall Tale

{Soliloquy Continued}
(Abana Fare)

I decide—
to use the fangs I hide.
And with all my might,
I bite and bite—
and rip and tear—
the weeds near.

Snap, the weed goes—
away from my nose.
Rip, rip, flee,
my arm is now free.
Yanking with nails,
my tail is now freed—
from every weed.

The many harsh weed,
that held me captive,
are now broken—
and forsaken.

Tall Tale

{Soliloquy Continued}
(Abana Fare)

I swim a ways,
away from haze.
My belly, hungry,
I sudden see,
not that far,
sardines and caviar.

So my stomach not hollow,
I chew and swallow.
Seems to me—
this meal is tasty.
I enjoy salty,
fresh seafood.
This is my food,
a mermaid's buffet—
in these waters lay.

With hand on my hip,
a gasp slip…

Tall Tale

{Soliloquy Continued}
(Abana Fare)

I also eye near—
seaweed floating there;
dark forest-green,
shiny, long, lean,
cold, damp, raw,
held in my claw,
I eat it raw.

Delicious, sour, tart…,
I tear it apart.
"I eat everything—
in sight," I sing…

Now finished with din,
I use a napkin.

The sea holds my heart,
tart…

Tall Tale

{Soliloquy Continued}
(Abana Fare)

…even when apart—
from my lover,
Ulder.

Despite my lovesick nature,
I find mystery—
in the hour—
now getting darker,
soothing my eyes—
with its dim atmosphere,
held dear.

Nights in the *Atlantic*,
I deem, "Terrific!"
Beyond aquatic,
I find it exotic—
with irresistible charm,
despite it often alarm.

Tall Tale

{Soliloquy Continued}
(Abana Fare)

No matter eyes shun,
danger in ocean—
is a notion—
that I'm drawn to.
Unable to resist its thrill,
I've not much will.

Ahead,
I now spot seafaring—
mermen, holding—
pitchforks and wearing—
a painted frown...

I turn upside down—
and speed away—
so they—
not ruin my day.

I keep swimming and fleeing...

Tall Tale

{Soliloquy Continued}
(Abana Fare)

Much further away,
they are "out of my way."
Now I turn right side up.

I conjure a cup—
of water icy—
and drink it quickly.

Then, "in a hurry,"
I swim speedy,
encountering shady—
territory;
area with much barnacle—
and many sharp icicle.

Ouch! I fear—
I've been cut here—
with tail bled.

Tall Tale

{Soliloquy Continued}
(Abana Fare)

Stricken dread,
I call, "Distress—
and bloody mess."

Moments pass—
and alas—
arrives "Neptune,"
deified, whistling tune,
offering assistance—
with a caring glance.

I mumble, "Yelp,
please help!"

He now wraps kelp—
around my wound bled—
and sprinkles table salt—
mixed with malt...

Tall Tale

{Soliloquy Continued}
(Abana Fare)

Grateful, I said,
"Oh God,
you're not odd."
Then I nod,
"Your image is art,
held in my heart,
adoration meant."

Sincere, I comment,
"God,
thank you—
for my rescue."

Neptune,
"Under the moon,
I shall pray to you—
with eyes woo,
brand-new."

Tall Tale

{Storyteller}
(Venus Fly)

As Abana appreciate,
she not consider fate,
nor worry about the clock—
and each tick tock.

Certain,
she's brave;
fears not a wave,
nor another mermaid's claw.
Moving her jaw,
she prefers her fish raw.
And has not much flaw.

Even she mend—
her "tail cloth," patches tend,
sewn by needle & thread;
stitched using gold spool—
and fabric wool.

Chapter Three

"ABANA AND ULDER"

Tall Tale

{Storyteller}
(Venus Fly)

Standing aloof,
my water-proof—
clock I'd wound…

Touching sandy ground,
Ulder's heart Abana found,
both soft-spoken.

But quiet is sudden—
broken—
by thunder,
creating a mood,
I brood,
of dark interlude—
and romance,
perchance.
His look,
not mistook,
shone love.

Tall Tale

{Storyteller Continued}
(Venus Fly)

Their rendezvous sweet,
Abana's heartbeat—
went, "thump"—
and Ulder felt "a lump—
in his throat."
The couple converse…

{Expressed to Ulder}
(Abana Fare)

For our romantic scene,
I offer a leaf green,
a token meant well.

I've waited by day—
for all I've to say.
I've waited by night—
to imagine you right,
handsome with tall height.

Tall Tale

{Expressed to Ulder Continued}
(Abana Fare)

Closing eyelids shadowed blue,
I dreamt of you—
just to get by—
all alone, I sigh.

And here you are—
near, not far,
brighter than any star.

Ulder, my lips—
have sunk ships—
and uttered charms.

Now held in your arms,
my lips kiss yours.

Above, the rain pours…
I ask, "Will you stay—
past dusk today?"

Tall Tale

{Expressed to Abana Fare}
(Ulder)

'Till swept away,
with you, I'll stay.

{Expressed to Ulder}
(Abana Fare)

"Swept away," you say.
What does sweep?
The tears I weep—
or restless sleep,
tossing—
and turning…?

{Expressed to Abana Fare}
(Ulder)

'Tis the seals,
that I prepare meals.
"Their cries," sense I.

Tall Tale

{Expressed to Abana Fare Continued}
(Ulder)

They need me,
sorry.
Although not grand,
please understand.

{Expressed to Ulder}
(Abana Fare)

Then let's not waste—
our time in haste.
Although I grow weak,
your love I still seek.
Come to my lair,
where we can share—
each need—
upon my bed of seaweed…

I live in a spot obscure,
reminiscent of folklore...

Tall Tale

{Expressed to Ulder Continued}
(Abana Fare)

We'll sped.
It's only minutes ahead.
Just beyond the reef white,
"hidden from sight!"

{Storyteller}
(Venus Fly)

Her hand in his,
fizz,
they swim fast.
Moments later,
each lover—
arrives at her shelter.

{Expressed to Ulder}
(Abana Fare)

I'll open the door…

Tall Tale

{Expressed to Ulder Continued}
(Abana Fare)

Come in, I'll give you a tour.
An antique collector,
there's an old trunk—
and oil-lamp in the corner,
rusted,
I dread…
Classic tables from—
shipwrecks stolen, I hum,
secured with bolts.

My coin collection there…
and diamond chandelier!
Antique plates and silverware,
even old-fashioned tankards.
And yards—
of fabrics upholstered,
adorning sofas and—
other furniture, grand.
Even shells on sand!

Tall Tale

{Expressed to Ulder Continued}
(Abana Fare)

The junk,
that seamen have sunk,
has become my treasure…

{Expressed to Abana Fare}
(Ulder)

Be it work or leisure,
"What's your pleasure?"

{Expressed to Ulder}
(Abana Fare)

Your strong arms—
and all of your charms—
in bed with me—
in salty sea.
Nobody will find us,
I fuss.

Tall Tale

{Expressed to Ulder Continued}
(Abana Fare)

Come,
here's my bed of seaweed,
I hum…
The sheets are full of moss.
On my lips I smear lip gloss.
"Make yourself comfortable."

{Storyteller}
(Venus Fly)

The two jump into bed,
on the pillow rests Ulder's head.
Abana's hair let down—
compliments her nightgown,
a pale yellow,
her eyes on her fellow…
Silhouetted by shade,
they become lovers—
under mossy covers…

Tall Tale

{Storyteller Continued}
(Venus Fly)

Seaweed for blanket—
and plump pillow set,
luxury the couple get—
as moans beget…,
"one lover to another."

Ulder now whisper…

{Expressed to Abana Fare}
(Ulder)

The moments we share…
Abana in bed, bare,
close to me, near.
Not a bother, nor strife,
soon you'll be my wife,
waltzing down the aisle,
you with smile…

Tall Tale

{Expressed to Ulder}
(Abana Fare)

Now you're mine,
a valentine…
With each moment—
shared, benevolent,
our amour lent…

{Expressed to Abana Fare}
(Ulder)

Part fish, we not hesitate—
as we mate…

{Storyteller}
(Venus Fly)

The couple especial bond,
both fond—
of their "hidden pond."

Tall Tale

{Storyteller Continued}
(Venus Fly)

The afternoon now gone,
they dress and,
"Sigh," grand.

To her mate, she relate…

{Expressed to Ulder}
(Abana Fare)

"Look, lover,
hung from my dresser:
a sailor's uniform—
found in a storm,
ragged and torn—
and no longer worn.
You may have it.
You could bring it—
to a seamstress—
to alter, I guess."

Tall Tale

{Storyteller}
(Venus Fly)

Ulder opens a trunk,
finding mostly junk.
And then he aware—
a wedding gown there!
"Olden and yellowed,"
he bellowed.

{Expressed to Abana Fare}
(Ulder)

"Who originally owned?"

{Expressed to Ulder}
(Abana Fare)

I not know.
I found it on the ground somewhere.
Would I wear—
with stains and sheer?

Tall Tale

{Expressed to Abana Fare}
(Ulder)

I'd marry you still,
whatever you will…

{Storyteller}
(Venus Fly)

The couple awhile stare—
and then dare—
to leave her lair.

Swimming afar, "hand—
held hand,"
they behold nature.
Then, they rest,
enjoying each other best…

Abana quest…

Chapter Four

"Lover's Rock"

Tall Tale

{Expressed to Ulder}
(Abana Fare)

Pleasant the smell of clover...,
but then—
something I wonder:
is it thunder,
Ulder,
or my heart—
falling apart?

{Expressed to Abana Fare}
(Ulder)

When we're together,
I'm sure it's the weather.
Fear not its sound,
nor the vibrations on ground.
The thunder's roar—
can't harm us here,
no matter your frightful stare.

Tall Tale

{Expressed to Ulder}
(Abana Fare)

And the lightning,
Darling?

{Expressed to Abana Fare}
(Ulder)

It sparks bright—
when in sight.
But with us underwater,
it can't bother—
our love affair,
nor tangle your hair,
that falls in curls—
and swirls,
and gently captivate.
The storm will abate—
upon its fate—
while we wait...

Tall Tale

{Expressed to Ulder}
(Abana Fare)

Although it enthrall,
I'd rather fall—
into your embrace,
touching your face—
and whispering,
"Grace."

{Storyteller}
(Venus Fly)

Another roar,
boom, the thunder—
cracks and lightning—
flashes a light glare,
brightening everywhere,
even miles under.

Again, the thunder—
holler...!

Tall Tale

{Storyteller Continued}
(Venus Fly)

Various sea creatures scare,
"What's going on here?"
As they hide behind—
bushes, their teeth grind…

Abana and Ulder,
feeling body-heat warm,
"weather the storm."

Ulder comforts her—
as he reassure,
"They're safer than those—
on shore."

Lightning accompanies—
the thunder's doom,
another crack, boom!

Abana now decides to groom…

Tall Tale

{Expressed to Ulder}
(Abana Fare)

I comb my hair…
It gets tangled, I fret.
And then I regret—
my locks in knots.

My comb's teeth rip—
strands as I grip.
Pull and pull, tear…
Locks of my hair—
in a chunk—
have then sunk.

"Ulder,
let's swim—
to shallow docks—
where we may brush—
a gush—
of rocks and shells,"
my tongue tells…

Tall Tale

{Storyteller}
(Venus Fly)

The couple swim—
in waters dim,
approaching shallow docks,
where found large rocks—
on sandy bottom,
I hum…

Ten minutes…,
goes the clock,
now at the dock…

Abana fixes a hairdo,
but still holds rue.
Ulder kisses her hand,
while "sweeping sand."

They share—
their time there…

Tall Tale

{Storyteller Continued}
(Venus Fly)

Again, goes the clock…,
another hour,
spent a bit sour.
Still at the docks,
Abana expresses her predicament—
with candor lent…

{Expressed to Ulder}
(Abana Fare)

I tightly tied—
my locks which fall aside.

{Expressed to Abana Fare}
(Ulder)

You still have a face—
prettier than lace,
even shows grace.

Tall Tale

{Expressed to Abana Fare Continued}
(Ulder)

Forever,
"your significant other,"
Ulder.

{Expressed to Ulder}
(Abana Fare)

If we become distant,
"on our own," I meant,
here, at these docks,
we can rendezvous,
where not one knew.

Else on shore of sea,
look for me—
and I'll appear—
before you, near,
combing my hair…

Tall Tale

{Expressed to Ulder Continued}
(Abana Fare)

I ask of you,
"Is it not true—
you want me too?"

{Expressed to Abana Fare}
(Ulder)

'Tis true, I want—
as ghosts will haunt,
desiring a heart to take. . .

{Expressed to Ulder}
(Abana Fare)

Like a flame, hot,
you're caught—
in my hair,
that I let down near.

Tall Tale

{Expressed to Ulder Continued}
(Abana Fare)

Tossing few strand—
around your shoulder,
deeming you, "my lover,"
I quiver.

Embracing at shallow docks,
"sun-spun locks"—
curl, bounce and flip.
Biting my lip,
one hand on my hip,
I conjure a love potion—
for your consumption.
You drink it,
tasting winter pine…
Now you're mine!
Given you—
a love-spell brew,
I must've had,
although it's sad…

Tall Tale

{Expressed to Ulder Continued}
(Abana Fare)

The pains in my heart—
whenever we part…

Under starlight—
on some dark night,
let's swim—
with moonlight dim.

And see skin where,
freckled and fair,
glows a red tint.

In your sleep,
my heart you keep.
In my wake,
your heart I take.

Ulder, lets swim to—
"Lover's Rock."

Tall Tale

{Storyteller}
(Venus Fly)

Abana & Ulder—
swim quickly under,
"out of the way."
Past the beach,
each—
hand around the clock—
moves, tick tock,
as they arrive at—
"Lover's Rock,"
a large boulder,
which one may behold—
in ways bold—
as it hold—
a lamp golden…

They sat upon the rock—
for two hours around the clock…
Abana—
desired to stay longer…

Tall Tale

{Storyteller Continued}
(Venus Fly)

And Ulder,
waving, departs,
to attend seals—
and offer meals…
And Abana,
awhile waits for pigeons—
to flock—
on top of the rock,
"Lover's Rock."

She splashes seawater—
on her face and neck,
feeling like a wreck.
"My lover gone,"
she sing,
high pitched.
Till dusk she'll stay—
when sunray—
go away…

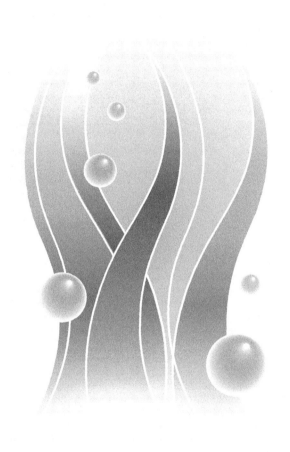

Chapter Five

"BORN FROM FICTION"

Tall Tale

{Storyteller Continued}
(Venus Fly)

Abana spots a seaman.
As he approach, looking lost,
she accost…

{Expressed to Fisherman}
(Abana Fare)

I'm born from fiction,
a mermaid in ocean,
but two legs upon land,
however grand…

{Expressed to Abana Fare}
(Fisherman)

Mermaid, bear with me.
"Bad English," oops!
Me speak poorly,
me no education, eh sorry.

Tall Tale

{Expressed to Abana Fare Continued}
(Fisherman)

But me fisherman,
I says whatever I can.
An me break grammar rule.
Me no fool.
Me no wanna speak like slave.
Rules of grammar pave—
an early grave,
enslaving speaker—
and even preacher.
Nose body tell me—
how for to speak clearly.
Me gonna chat—
anyhow wrong at that.
Me no care…
if me goin' nose where.
Know where I'm to dwell?
Me no go to hell.
An me no slave to English.
Me eats fish.

Tall Tale

{Expressed to Abana Fare Continued}
(Fisherman)

Me spit out each word—
you've heard.
Me butcher the English Language.
An then me say, "No baggage."

"Don't judge a cover by its book"—
cuz can mistook—
the picture of the book.

"Don't make a mole-hill—
out of a mountain!"

Me no need church pew.
"Something borrowed, something blue,"
never do me say, "I do."

Never do me kiss the bride.
Instead, I look and hide!

Tall Tale

{Expressed to Fisherman}
(Abana Fare)

Amused,
you've one wish—
from the eyes of a fish.
My head tilts lazily…
And what might it be?

{Expressed to Abana Fare}
(Fisherman)

Me present one wish—
from me mermaid fish.
I hold my heart queerly—
an smile gaily!
What's ah deal!
And so I feel—
it good for me—
to take your sea—
and wish you be—
in this lamp, see…

Tall Tale

{Expressed to Fisherman}
(Abana Fare)

And where will this—
lamp stay until a kiss—
warms your heart?

{Expressed to Abana Fare}
(Fisherman)

You will not part—
from this here rock,
trapped in this lamp, tock.
Whoever rubs it,
frees you of it.

{Expressed to Fisherman}
(Abana Fare)

Oh… like a jinn—
or a genie within…

Tall Tale

{Expressed to Fisherman Continued}
(Abana Fare)

And are you sure—
that's your wish, sir?

{Expressed to Abana Fare}
(Fisherman)

As sure as the sea—
that offers to me—
a place for to fish,
that is my wish.

{Expressed to Fisherman}
(Abana Fare)

As you wish, Sir.
I'll grant this, sure,
with a spell—
that should work swell.

Tall Tale

{Expressed to Fisherman Continued}
(Abana Fare)

This lamp of gold—
antique sold,
be my new home—
where I shan't roam.

As I turn into—
smoke, I tell you:
this lamp I go inside—
so that I may hide.
So long! Farewell!

{Soliloquy}
(Fisherman)

Gentle, I tell,
half well,
so she—
understand me.

Tall Tale

{Soliloquy Continued}
(Fisherman)

My English is—
bad, it is,
gees.
Why sorry for this.
Me mermaid, I miss,
I explain you…

So you don't meet—
men to greet,
I wished you in lamp.
You not too cramp.
You're a genie—
who wait for me—
to return from sea.
I go catch clam—
an trade it for ham.
I fish oyster—
an trade it for moister—
red meat.

Tall Tale

{Soliloquy Continued}
(Fisherman)

I likes sweet.
I works hard for—
to trap lobster,
scallops, shrimp, crab.
Seafood I grab.
I catch a lot.
Then it's bought—
in trade—
for homemade—
apple pie;
steak to fry;
beef and potato stew;
spice and potatoes—
for under my nose;
much of onions and more—
at post or cheap store—
by de back door.

Work me must!

Tall Tale

{Soliloquy Continued}
(Fisherman)

Me do lust—
me mermaid,
But me must trade!

Nobody find me mermaid.
Nobody swim here.
Swim more near—
the sea's shore.
Yes, me sure!

Me wave, good-bye,
and I now say, bye—
to me mermaid.

Mermaid, I go fish.
Thanks for the wish!
Bye, bye, mermaid.
Me must trade!

Tall Tale

{Storyteller}
(Venus Fly)

The seaman afar does fade.
Trapped in a lamp, Abana,
in human form—
with legs, did transform.
There she does wait,
cursing her fate...

Chapter Six

"Lamp of Olden Days"

Tall Tale

{Soliloquy}
(Abana Fare)

A tail is grand—
in water, on sand.
But legs on land—
attract a mate,
who won't hesitate.

Being so small,
I transformed into human,
counterpart of man.
My limbs sore—
matter not more.

I've become a bore—
trapped in a lamp,
dark and damp,
a fate of ill,
waiting until—
a man frees me—
and returns me to sea.

Tall Tale

{Soliloquy Continued}
(Abana Fare)

And then I recall—
most of all—
an Arabian tale,
which I feel—
befits this situation—
with similar notion;
i.e.,
"Genie in Bottle,"
trapped as I wait—
for one strong,
who shan't "rub me wrong."

If one "rubs me the wrong way,"
then no "light of day,"
nor sea, nor bay.

If rub the lamp right,
then I'd be freed,
An honorable deed!

Tall Tale

{Soliloquy Continued}
(Abana Fare)

Which will it be?
A free genie—
    or not?

Am I to rot—
in this forsaken—
lamp of olden?

{Storyteller}
(Venus Fly)

As time ticks on,
now low tide gone,
Abana feels cramp—
stuck in the lamp.

Now with each—
    tick tock…,

Tall Tale

{Storyteller Continued}
(Venus Fly)

…my wound clock—
spells, "six o'clock."
And in the distance,
brews a new romance—
as a sailor spots—
the lamp, anticipating—
"a genie sewing,"
stitching her cloth—
how she doth…

The seaman reaches—
the lamp and says,
"I rub the lamp sudden,
again and again…"

{Expressed to Abana Fare}
(Seaman)

Now before my sight…,

Tall Tale

{Expressed to Abana Fare Continued}
(Seaman)

…in the air,
smoke does appear.
Misty gray gust—
turns to dust—
as a girl appear,
drawing me near…
Young girl,
I offer you a pearl—
and the waters I sail—
just to feel—
alive at sea.

{Expressed to Seaman}
(Abana Fare)

You've rescued me!
Thank you, sir.
Your name?

Tall Tale

{Expressed to Abana Fare}
(Seaman)

My name is "Seaman."
You seem rather coy,
shining like a star.
And you are?

{Expressed to Seaman}
(Abana Fare)

My name is Abana Fare.
Please, forgive my stare.

{Expressed to Abana Fare}
(Seaman)

As you twirl,
I see you're a girl…?
Or a lady—
reserved, shady…?

Tall Tale

{Expressed to Seaman}
(Abana Fare)

I'm no girl.
I am a mermaid,
past school grade.

{Expressed to Abana Fare}
(Seaman)

But you've legs!

{Expressed to Seaman}
(Abana Fare)

Born from fiction,
I took human form—
to weather the storm.

You appear curious,
I fuss…

Tall Tale

{Expressed to Abana Fare}
(Seaman)

Can you change back?

{Expressed to Seaman}
(Abana Fare)

With a puff of smoke black—
and a wink,
I will my tail back!
And now you see—
a mermaid from sea.

And yourself, glee,
gazing at thee…

{Expressed to Abana Fare}
(Seaman)

I've much hap,
I clap…

Tall Tale

{Expressed to Abana Fare Continued}
(Seaman)

A mermaid from sea—
beckons me!

{Expressed to Seaman}
(Abana Fare)

Enchantment in me,
my will be.
From heart of fish,
I grant any wish…

Be it afar,
even a star—
I plunder will be yours.

The precipitation pours.
Captivated,
"my hand yours."

Tall Tale

{Expressed to Abana Fare}
(Seaman)

Then I wish us afloat,
there, in my boat.

{Expressed to Seaman}
(Abana Fare)

Wink,
and here—
we are—
with land afar.

{Expressed to Abana Fare}
(Seaman)

Then I wish us land—
on shores of sand,
where splash seawater—
and seashells abound—
on ground.

Tall Tale

{Expressed to Seaman}
(Abana Fare)

Wink,
here's your sand—
upon the land.

{Expressed to Abana Fare}
(Seaman)

You've much magic,
full of trick.
You just wink,
and then we're here,
close to town near,
where I live.

To you I give—
my heart and more—
of shallow and deep.
My heart you may keep.

Tall Tale

{Expressed to Seaman}
(Abana Fare)

"My heart yours"—
as the tide soars,
wetting the sand—
upon which we stand.

"And when high tide—
submerge," I chide,
"with heart hide,
I'll afar swim—
with sunlight dim—
into depths of chill,
waiting until—
shallow waters become—
where I'll emerge," I hum,
"rolling ashore,
craving you once more."

We'll embrace again.

Tall Tale

{Expressed to Seaman Continued}
(Abana Fare)

And I'll say then,
"How have you been?"
Our eyes shall see…,
still, you love me.

Lonely not more,
whispering on shore,
"What's romance for?"

{Expressed to Abana Fare}
(Seaman)

To enjoy and get—
none of regret.

Excuse me…,
I'm thirsty—
for water icy.

Tall Tale

{Expressed to Seaman}
(Abana Fare)

Wink, here's your ice water.
I drink from the sea—
cause I like it salty.

Salt of sea—
now inside me!
It soothes my scales—
and bones it heals…

{Expressed to Abana Fare}
(Seaman)

I wish you legs on land,
wherever you stand.

{Expressed to Seaman}
(Abana Fare)

Wink, now 'tis true.

Tall Tale

{Expressed to Abana Fare}
(Seaman)

Excuse me,
I swallow more sips…

{Expressed to Seaman}
(Abana Fare)

With cold fingertips,
against my lips,
a whisper slips…,
"Loose lips sink ships."

{Expressed to Abana Fare}
(Seaman)

Fond of you,
I never tire—
from the light glare—
in your soft hair…

Tall Tale

{Expressed to Seaman}
(Abana Fare)

Our mood glad,
wherever we may gad.
If feelings not had—
our romance could wait,
I hesitate…

{Expressed to Abana Fare}
(Seaman)

I wish us abed…

{Storyteller}
(Venus Fly)

Abana, with legs crossed—
and long locks tossed,
covers his lips—
with one finger.
Awhile his desire linger…

Tall Tale

{Storyteller Continued}
(Venus Fly)

With a wink, they abed—
under sheets red,
in his bed…
While rain,
against the windowpane,
adds ambiance…

Abana whisper,
"Upon land I've no other—
lover."
Still, she crave—
the saltwater…

After their romance,
Abana is beset by hindrance;
her aching legs and feet sore—
caused her an unwanted bore.
She must will her tail back!

Tall Tale

{Storyteller Continued}
(Venus Fly)

Closing each eyelid,
the dim light hid…
Seeing only black,
Abana will her tail back,
explaining she must part—
although she held his heart.

With a long sigh—
and a wink of one eye,
she whisper,
"Good-bye."

{Soliloquy}
(Seaman)

She's gone from me,
back to sea…

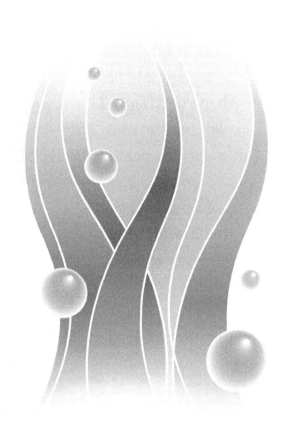

Chapter Seven

"SPECTACLE IN SEAWATER"

Tall Tale

{Storyteller}
(Venus Fly)

Be I,
Venus Fly,
"Ruler of Seas."
I wheeze,
"With fire in my hair,
I wound fools whom stare,
warning those who dare…"

Meanwhile, devoid cares,
the mermaid, Abana, appears—
where one fears—
danger in sea,
all around she…

Abana swims further,
searching for adventure.
But ventures too far.
Now in "shark infested"—
waters, she dread…

Tall Tale

{Storyteller Continued}
(Venus Fly)

Abana beholds sharks,
that communicate through sparks—
of sound waves and movement.

Now weary of where she went…,
she should've been vigilante—
or at least observant.

{Soliloquy}
(Abana Fare)

I aware "Blacktip,"
a shark who now sip.

Then I spot—
one who's not—
friendly with me—
in my ocean of sea,
where waves adore me…

Tall Tale

{Soliloquy Continued}
(Abana Fare)

This shark is uncouth.
Goes by the name, "Narrowtooth."
He declares me—
his enemy—
through sound waves.

He paves—
a way to terrorize—
through blackened eyes.

He uses "Morse Code"—
with seeds,
pebbles and weeds;
he draw—
while using his jaw…

But I don't know "Morse Code."
And I should've swum to my abode.

Tall Tale

{Soliloquy Continued}
(Abana Fare)

In prayer, my hands I now hold.

The Narrowtooth Shark circles around—
my aquatic ground—
with an expression I not mistook,
emitting a deadly look.

A paramour or knight I need—
if I'm not to bleed—
to death,
expiring upon my last breath.

The Narrowtooth Shark's angry stare—
scares me more than I can bear.
Shaken and consumed with fear,
I become reticent.

"The shark's teeth are fatal,"
I tell.

Tall Tale

{Soliloquy Continued}
(Abana Fare)

Just a mermaid, I've not a chance—
with neither spear nor lance,
nor way to seduce a romance.

Narrowtooth is immune to my charms—
as his look alarms.

My arm wrapped in sea kelp,
desperate, I call for help,
"SOS."

My plea, do not shun,
even if you're expecting someone!
Save me from his bite,
and you, I'll love tonight.

"Low & Behold,"
I bite my lip.
Here comes "Blacktip!"

Tall Tale

{Soliloquy Continued}
(Abana Fare)

To rescue a "damsel in distress,"
"Blacktip" cares about me,
obviously.

The "Blacktip" shark fends off—
"Narrowtooth" as I run off;
and quickly swim—
away from him!

The "Narrowtooth" killer—
is more than a thriller!
And now past a coral reef,
I'm over my grief!

Swimming where none fear,
I see an octopus near...,
behind strands of my hair,
which float wild in sea—
in front of me.

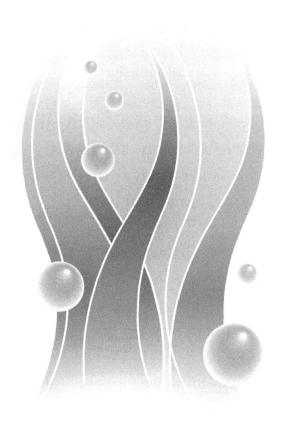

Chapter Eight

"HER FIGURE CLAD"

Tall Tale

{Storyteller}
(Venus Fly)

Abana, crafty,
seeks safety—
in waters marked territory—
for mermaids, mermen—
and their children.

Awhile swimming, she—
does spot—
an old necklace with rot.
She mumbles in soliloquy…

{Soliloquy}
(Abana Fare)

I deem it antique art:
shaped in a heart,
held by a chain broken,
some sort of token…

Tall Tale

{Soliloquy Continued}
(Abana Fare)

The ocean, dark and cold,
held the stone I now hold.

Its blue gemstone,
sparkling appearance shone,
shines crystal with luster…

Oops! It slips—
from my fingertips,
now lost in the ocean—
of a mermaid's notion.

I resume—
swimming. And assume—
I know he,
whom I spot in front of me…

Squinting, I see—
an old friend, "Sabni."

Tall Tale

{Storyteller}
(Venus Fly)

Abana and Sabni—
stop and chat—
about "this & that"…

Sabni mentions a seamstress,
who alters dress—
and stitches hat, cloak,
blouse & miniskirt—
for whomever flirt…

{Expressed to Abana Fare}
(Sabni)

The seamstress enjoys fame,
"Abrianna," her name.
She can sew—
you a top of yellow!
She stitches quick,
any fabric pick…

Tall Tale

{Expressed to Abana Fare Continued}
(Sabni)

Nudity make not one smart,
nor polite for tart—
cookies and tea—
in the busy sea!
There floats lobsters, sharks and cod—
and largely more and 'tis odd—
that mermaids feel the sea—
is a nudist colony!
There's even schools of fish.
I wish—
you wear new fashion—
in the public ocean!

{Expressed to Sabni}
(Abana Fare)

I'm a mermaid!
Mermaids swim topless—
since born, more or less!

Tall Tale

{Expressed to Abana Fare}
(Sabni)

No, that must change—
or you'll look strange.
Come, we go find her,
Abrianna…
She not far from here.

{Storyteller}
(Venus Fly)

Sabni and Abana swim, where seek,
"Abrianna's Boutique."
Minutes later,
they join her…

Sabni tells the seamstress—
that his friend's figure—
needs cloth to clad—
her nakedness,
a top or party dress.

Tall Tale

{Storyteller Continued}
(Venus Fly)

Sabni introduces Abrianna—
to Abana,
and begs for assistance…

{Introduces Females}
(Sabni)

Abrianna,
meet Abana.
We're here because—
she swims topless—
cause says "she's a mermaid."

{Expressed to Abana Fare}
(Abrianna)

Oh! I've got—
a top that ought—
to look swell…

Tall Tale

{Storyteller}
(Venus Fly)

Abana tries on the garment—
with polite sentiment…

{Expressed to Abrianna}
(Abana Fare)

Covers my skin,
once bare,
with a flare—
for a flimsy—
top called a bikini!

I adore the new fashion—
for the "public ocean."
I thank you much,
modeling as such…

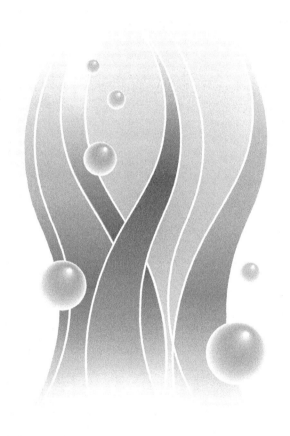

Chapter Nine

"Confronts a Foe"

Tall Tale

{Storyteller}
(Venus Fly)

Abana, swimming fast,
finds her familiar rock at last.

{Soliloquy}
(Abana Fare)

I spot candy—
on the rock, dandy!
I climb on it—
and gather a bit—
of what seamen left behind.
Chewing, my teeth grind.

Finished with my treat,
thump, my heart beat...

Lonely,
"the keeper of the sea"—
that waits for me...

Tall Tale

{Soliloquy Continued}
(Abana Fare)

Moments I bide—
until I ride—
the waves of sea—
that beckon me…

{Storyteller}
(Venus Fly)

In haste she sway,
searching for prey.
Instead, she encounters a merman.
Or more precise, a madman!
An archenemy, Ambrose is a foe,
who causes Abana much woe…

{Expressed to Abana Fare}
(Ambrose)

Full is your lip.

Tall Tale

{Expressed to Abana Fare Continued}
(Ambrose)

But then here's a tip—
about gossip—
that ends—
your lovers and friends.

Malevolent rumors I spread—
until you dread—
your beau no more,
alone on seashore.

{Expressed to Ambrose}
(Abana Fare)

Ambrose,
you're gross.
Can't you see—
I search the sea—
to catch prey for me?

Tall Tale

{Expressed to Abana Fare}
(Ambrose)

That's all you'll search for—
when a lover, you've no more,
alone forevermore—
once I slander you and lie—
to every single guy.

{Expressed to Ambrose}
(Abana Fare)

I shan't rue.
None of it's true!
Who will believe you?

{Expressed to Abana Fare}
(Ambrose)

Ulder, Sabni and Matt.
How 'bout that?

Tall Tale

{Expressed to Ambrose}
(Abana Fare)

Biting my lip,
I ask,
"What's the gossip?"

{Expressed to Abana Fare}
(Ambrose)

I speak trash rather well.
All I'll tell:
You adore eels—
cause you like how each feels—
and you contracted a disease—
because you are a sleaze.

{Expressed to Ambrose}
(Abana Fare)

They won't believe it.
Hence, I not care a bit.

Tall Tale

{Expressed to Abana Fare}
(Ambrose)

I'll add:
It's rather sad—
that you also welcome snails—
cause you think each feels—
rather warm—
and you've got a tapeworm—
inside you as well.
That's what I'm gonna tell.

{Expressed to Ambrose}
(Abana Fare)

Ambrose, why?
Why do this? I sigh.

{Expressed to Abana Fare}
(Ambrose)

Cause you swum off…

Tall Tale

{Expressed to Abana Fare Continued}
(Ambrose)

…and shouted, I cough,
that the one and only Ambrose—
is plain and simply gross.
You did that, I hiss.
Now I am gonna do this!

{Expressed to Ambrose}
(Abana Fare)

You plan, scheme,
to ruin my dream.
You'll fail, I deem.
You'll drown before—
you say anymore.

{Expressed to Abana Fare}
(Ambrose)

I'm going to find…

Tall Tale

{Expressed to Abana Fare Continued}
(Ambrose)

… your lovers, no mind—
me, and also every shark—
you meet after dark!

I'll tell all!
And melancholy will befall—
upon you, and you'll sleep—
with me, else weep—
everyday—
away—
and be troubled by most,
and even a ghost!

{Expressed to Ambrose}
(Abana Fare)

You're a "loony bell!"
And this I tell:
I'm hungry for food.

Tall Tale

{Expressed to Ambrose Continued}
(Abana Fare)

And that you, crude,
cause me hunger pains—
and stains—
of dread!
With you I shan't bed.
And as for my skin,
even on my shin,
you will not touch!
My eyes such—
can wound you much!
"Don't keep in touch."

Disappear—
afore my stare!
You needn't be near—
to spit out lies.
And "no long good-byes."
I tell you like so:
Just go!

Tall Tale

{Expressed to Abana Fare}
(Ambrose)

I'll sing, "Hey, everybody—
in the sea,
Abana welcomes eels—
and snails—
and has a disease—
on her knees—
and everywhere too—
cause the entire custodial crew—
she said, "Hello," to—
turned green mold—
and quickly grew old.

{Expressed to Ambrose}
(Abana Fare)

They'll never believe—
and you'll grieve—
when you turn old—
with unmistaken mold!

Tall Tale

{Expressed to Abana Fare}
(Ambrose)

From my lips, "trash,"
telling, "you also got a rash."

{Expressed to Ambrose}
(Abana Fare)

With ailment I contend.
I needn't "gossip bend,"
nor garbage—
from the sewage.
Your each insult—
need halt!

Nobody would ever—
believe it clever!
You haven't a reason to complain.
You won't succeed causing me bane,
nor ruin my reputation,
nor make others shun!

Tall Tale

{Expressed to Ambrose Continued}
(Abana Fare)

I'll destroy you and spit.
I'm just sick of it!
The madder I become,
the hungrier I get,
I hum.

{Expressed to Abana Fare}
(Ambrose)

The "stars hold fate,"
wanna date?

{Expressed to Ambrose}
(Abana Fare)

No! I must procure—
food before I tire—
with much ire.

Tall Tale

{Storyteller}
(Venus Fly)

Ambrose swims away,
proud he spoiled Abana's day…

{Soliloquy}
(Abana Fare)

He's gone now, a relief!
But still, I swim in grief—
beyond a coral reef,
past a sunken ship,
deeper I dip.

And in my ocean,
I've a notion—
of days to come…

Tears, I sigh,
fall from each eye,
in drips…

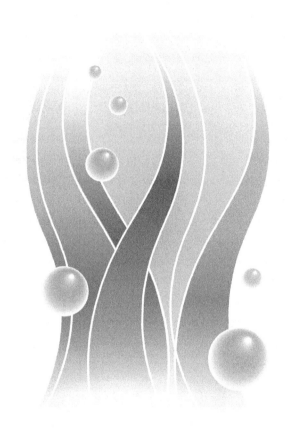

Chapter Ten

"Please, Fisherman!"

Tall Tale

{Soliloquy}
(Abana Fare)

I beckon you,
"man of crew,"
any fisherman—
to feed—
a ration I need—
to go on and live.
Lobster one may give.

"But where is the crew—
of this ship—
I see in front of me?"

The fish are sick.
Which ones to pick?
I'm starving,
fishermen!

I'm sore.
Rotten apple's core,

Tall Tale

{Soliloquy Continued}
(Abana Fare)

I can't complain more.
Can you not see?
I'm starving in sea!

I only need—
a bit of fish—
in my dish.
But the fish—
are all sick.
There's none to pick.

I've dismay in my heart.
I'll start—
to hunt for food,
even half-chewed.

I'll beg for tuna—
or cod,
"Oh my God!"

Tall Tale

{Soliloquy Continued}
(Abana Fare)

I must eat—
raw meat,
salty and sweet,
to satiate—
my need to eat!

I've aches and pains,
but mostly hunger pains.
I am growing weak.
Food I seek.

{Storyteller}
(Venus Fly)

Suddenly, a fisherman—
spots Abana begging for food.
So he not rude,
he throws her food.

Tall Tale

{Soliloquy}
(Abana Fare)

Now on my lips,
a really big fish—
for my dish.

I do tell:
I'll consume and be well.
My heart beats for you.
"Sir, much thank you."

{Storyteller}
(Venus Fly)

The fisherman waves—
to a mermaid he saves…
Abana now dine—
in saltwater,
tasting fish drenched with brine.

Chapter Eleven

"Venus Fly Concludes"

Tall Tale

{Storyteller}
(Venus Fly)

Upon a verge—
with nostalgic urge,
I quickly submerge—
to the bottom—
of the Atlantic,
seeking the horrific—
"Venus Flytrap Plant."

With eyes askant—
and heart yearn,
my tail I turn—
over a wild furn.
And then I spot—
that I sought,
its petals full bloom,
foreshadowing doom.

And here I groom,
tying my hair...

Tall Tale

{Storyteller Continued}
(Venus Fly)

…and fixing that I wear.

The plant bear—
seeds and nectar,
which I devour,
a bit sour.

Its juice rejuvenate—
in moments I wait,
leaving my skin silky—
and my complexion milky.

And now I daydream about a ball—
with fancy wear and all…,
accessories, gloves and jewelry—
and eye-shadow sugary.

My lips redden and shine,
glossed with brine.

Tall Tale

{Storyteller Continued}
(Venus Fly)

My emerald gown,
with highlights brown,
brushing the floor—
in green I'd wore.

But then I recall—
my tail tall—
and no party dress—
with disheveled locks, a mess!

No waltz, nor lover tall;
no royal castle hall;
no whispers, nor catcall;
no anybody at all!

Dismayed—
with dreams I bade…,
my fantasy now fade.

Tall Tale

{Storyteller Continued}
(Venus Fly)

Time wound,
soon I notice around,
where seaweed abound—
on the ground…

I clutch—
a bunch such,
wrapping a shawl…

"Good-bye," I drawl.
My pen now scrawl,
"The End."